Dracula

*Retold from the Bram Stoker original
by Tania Zamorsky*

Illustrated by Jamel Akib

Sterling Publishing Co., Inc.
New York

Library of Congress Cataloging-in-Publication Data

Zamorsky, Tania.
 Dracula / retold from the Bram Stoker original ; abridged by Tania Zamorsky ;
illustrated by Jamel Akib ; afterword by Arthur Pober.
   p. cm.—(Classic starts)
 Summary: Having discovered the double identity of the wealthy Transylvanian
nobleman, Count Dracula, a small group of people vow to rid the world of the
evil vampire.
 ISBN-13: 978-1-4027-3690-2
 ISBN-10: 1-4027-3690-8
 [1. Vampires—Fiction. 2. Horror stories.] I. Akib, Jamel, ill. II. Stoker, Bram,
1847–1912. Dracula. III. Title. IV. Series.

PZ7.Z25457Dr 2006
[Fic]—dc22

                                                                    2006005458

                     2 4 6 8 10 9 7 5 3 1

                  Published by Sterling Publishing Co., Inc.
               387 Park Avenue South, New York, NY 10016
                      Copyright © 2007 by Tania Zamorsky
                   Illustrations copyright © 2007 by Jamel Akib
                   Distributed in Canada by Sterling Publishing
                  ^c/_o Canadian Manda Group, 165 Dufferin Street,
                       Toronto, Ontario, Canada M6K 3H6
        Distributed in the United Kingdom by GMC Distribution Services,
        Castle Place, 166 High Street, Lewes, East Sussex, England BN7 1XU
          Distributed in Australia by Capricorn Link (Australia) Pty. Ltd.
                    P.O. Box 704, Windsor, NSW 2756, Australia

           Classic Starts is a trademark of Sterling Publishing Co., Inc.

                               Printed in China
                              All rights reserved

                   Sterling ISBN-13: 978-1-4027-3690-2
                        ISBN-10: 1-4027-3690-8

        For information about custom editions, special sales, premium and
            corporate purchases, please contact Sterling Special Sales
          Department at 800-805-5489 or specialsales@sterlingpub.com.

CONTENTS

CHAPTER 1

Jonathan Starts His Journey

ᴄᴏ

"Whooo!" went the whistle, and Jonathan Harker shut his eyes, allowing the romance and rhythm of the train to overtake him. He was traveling to Transylvania by rail to conduct some business with Count Dracula. Jonathan was a lawyer who worked for the firm of a Mr. Peter Hawkins. The firm was advising the count on the purchase of Carfax, a very old home in London.

Along the way to Transylvania, Jonathan visited Vienna, toured the streets of Budapest, strolled the splendid bridges over the Danube, and had an excellent supper of chicken paprika, a specialty of the region, at the Hotel Royale in Klausenburgh. For some reason he was very nervous. Although his bed at the hotel was comfortable enough, he had all sorts of strange dreams. *It must be the paprika*, he thought.

After more paprika for breakfast, this time in his porridge, Jonathan got back onto the train to continue his journey to the East. Looking out the windows, he saw a country that was full of beauty of every kind. There were streams, sweeping rivers, little towns, and the occasional castle on a hilltop. And at every station they passed there stood groups of interesting people, including women with full white sleeves and petticoats, and Slovakian men sporting heavy black mustaches, big cowboy hats, and enormous studded leather belts and boots.

It was twilight when the train arrived at Bistritz, in the Carpathian mountains. Count

Dracula had directed Jonathan to go to the Golden Krone Hotel, where he was expected. After greeting Jonathan at the door, the hotel's elderly landlady nervously handed him a note:

My friend, welcome. I am anxiously expecting you. Sleep well tonight, for tomorrow you will take the final leg of your journey, by carriage, to my castle. I trust that you will enjoy your stay in my beautiful land.

Your friend, Dracula.

"Do you know the count?" Jonathan asked the landlady. "Can you tell me anything about the castle?" But instead of answering him, the old woman simply crossed herself, handed over the room key, and hurried away.

Early the next morning, however, she knocked frantically on his door. "Oh! Young man," she cried, "must you go?"

Jonathan replied that indeed he must, for he had important business to conduct with the count.

"But don't you realize where you are going?" the landlady asked. "And on what day?" She didn't wait for answers. "It is the eve of Saint George Day. Tonight at midnight, all of the world's evil things will take control."

Jonathan tried to comfort the old woman, but it was no use. Finally, firmly, he repeated that he had a job to do, and would be continuing as planned on the last leg of his journey that night, by coach.

"Well, then at least take this, if only for your poor mother's sake." She took a crucifix from around her neck, and reached up and around to put it on his. Curiously, after the crucifix, she pressed tightly into his hand a head of garlic.

After she left, Jonathan took off the crucifix and looked at it. He considered throwing it away along with the garlic. An old churchman of England, he didn't really approve of or believe in such things. Feeling a strange, lingering uneasiness, however, he put the cross back around his neck.

When the coach arrived that evening, a small crowd quickly gathered around it. Carrying his bags, Jonathan walked past the coach driver, the elderly landlady, and some other hotel guests. All seemed to be staring at and discussing him.

In panicked and pitying whispers, they kept repeating the same word, *"Vrolok."* Upon opening up his little dictionary once he was seated in the coach, Jonathan learned it meant either "werewolf" or "vampire" in Serbian.

As the coach pulled away, Jonathan noticed many people in the now growing crowd making the sign of the cross. In his tiny journal, in which he recorded in shorthand everything that happened to him, Jonathan made a note to ask Count

Dracula about the townspeople's strange super-stitions. Jonathan wondered why even his fellow passengers were looking at him so sadly.

As they rode, the mountains and forests tow-ered around them in beautiful colors of deep blue and purple and green. As the sun began to sink, however, dark shadows and ghostlike clouds replaced that rainbow. And the darker it got, the more restless the driver and other passengers became.

"Can't you go any faster?" one passenger asked the driver, in a harsh whisper.

"I'm trying!" the driver wildly whispered back. Indeed, although they seemed to be mak-ing good time, the driver was obviously racing. Jonathan held on for dear life as the carriage rocked wildly on its springs.

As the coach approached the Borgo Pass, heavy thunder filled the sky. The driver and the other passengers craned over the edge of the coach, peering into the darkness, as though looking for something. Jonathan looked, too, but there was nothing and no one there.

"Too bad," the driver exclaimed. "The coach that was supposed to meet you to take you up to the castle is not here. You cannot wait here in the dark alone, as there are too many wolves about, and I must continue on. You will have to come with us. I can bring you back another time."

"Too bad," the other passengers murmured. But why did they all seem so cheerful?

"Not so fast," said a deep voice. A carriage driven by four coal-black horses pulled up alongside the coach. *This must be the count's assistant*, Jonathan thought. The man's face was mostly hidden by a great black hat, but Jonathan could see a pair of very bright eyes, glowing almost red. "You were extremely early tonight," the assistant told the driver, "but I anticipated your game. Now give me the gentleman's luggage."

CHAPTER 2

Jonathan Arrives at the Castle

∽

As the passengers continued to cross themselves, Jonathan said good-bye and climbed into the carriage. It was almost midnight. Remembering the landlady's words, he could not help but shiver at this, despite the blanket and hot tea that the count's assistant had offered him. His shivering only increased when, off in the distance, wolves began to howl. The horses seemed to be shivering, too, or at least snorting with fright.

Just then a cloud that had been covering the moon shifted, bathing the scene in a pale blue light. There, all around them, stood the wolves—creatures with white teeth and red tongues, long limbs and shaggy hair.

Jonathan jumped. It was terrifying to think that these creatures had been so close the entire time. But the count's assistant merely raised his arms and whispered something to the wolves, which fell immediately back. A cloud covered the moon again then, and they were once again in darkness.

The carriage climbed the remaining distance up the steep mountain to what Jonathan could now see was a vast and ruined castle. Through great round arches, they entered a dark courtyard and stopped.

The driver left Jonathan and his luggage at the castle's front door and then, with no further word or instruction, pulled away. The carriage disappeared into the night.

The huge front door was made of wood, and carved in great detail, but Jonathan could see no knocker or bell anywhere. Taking a step back and looking up at the castle's long black windows, he could not see even one ray of light.

Just then, from behind the door, he heard steps approaching. The steps were followed by the sounds of rattling chains and great steel bolts being pushed to the side. The door swung open and there stood a tall old man clad entirely in black, with gleaming eyes that looked strangely familiar. He had thick bushy eyebrows, pale skin, and very red lips. And when he smiled, behind those red lips were sharp-looking ivory teeth.

"Welcome to my castle," the man said, in excellent but heavily accented English. "I am Count Dracula." He reached out and shook Jonathan's hand.

Taking Jonathan's bags, the count led him

through long dark passages and up many wind-ing sets of stone stairs. *What grim adventure will this be?* Jonathan wondered as they walked. But when the count threw open the door to what would be his room, Jonathan was slightly relieved. There, before him, was a warm crackling fire in the hearth and a delicious dinner spread out on a nearby table.

I was silly to be afraid, Jonathan told himself sternly. *I have allowed the suspicions of the townspeople to get to me.* After all, he was a professional, here to do a job. He was also very hungry.

"Won't you be joining me?" he asked the count, noticing that only one place had been set for dinner.

"Oh, no," the count said. "I don't . . . I mean, I've already eaten."

The count stayed, however, and kept Jonathan company while he ate, asking him all sorts of questions.

"If a ship comes into an English port," the count asked, for example, "can I arrange for someone to come and pick up cargo and have it transported into town?"

"Of course," Jonathan said. "My firm could arrange that for you."

"What if I wanted to arrange it myself?" the count asked. "No offense. I trust you will understand that sometimes it is wise to spread out your affairs, and not have one person knowing all of your business."

Jonathan gave the count the names of some firms that could take care of such matters.

Only as the first dim strand of the morning sun came through the window of Jonathan's room did the count stand up and push back his chair. Somewhere in the valley below, distant wolves began to howl.

Jonathan shivered, thinking back to the awful creatures that had lined the carriage's path. The count, however, smiled. "Listen to them," he said, almost wistfully. "The children of the night."

Jonathan shivered even more, not only at this strange comment but at something else he noticed just then—the count's strangely hairy hands, with long thin fingernails cut to a sharp, almost clawlike point.

Things would be clearer, he hoped, in the morning.

CHAPTER 3

Jonathan Learns He Is a Prisoner

⌒

Jonathan slept late into the next day. When he awoke, the count was gone. In addition to another fine meal, which Jonathan would eat alone, the count had left a note. It encouraged Jonathan to go anywhere he liked in the castle, except into those rooms whose doors were locked.

"And you must never," the note stressed, strangely, "fall asleep anywhere else in the castle, except in your own room!"

Jonathan worked most of the day on the

count's property purchase. Needing a break, however, he decided that he would explore a bit. The castle was like a museum, he thought, marveling at the antiques, art, and other collectibles, all of the finest quality, and most of which seemed to be hundreds of years old.

In all of his wanderings, however, there were two things Jonathan did not see. The first thing missing was other people. *How can the count not have anyone to help him in this huge castle?* he wondered. The other thing missing, he noticed, was mirrors, even in the bathrooms. He was not vain, mind you, but a mirror did come in handy sometimes, such as when shaving. Thankfully, he had brought his own, a small compact, part of his traveling toiletry kit.

The count came home that evening after dark and their routine continued. The count never ate, always claiming to have already eaten, and instead just kept Jonathan company, going over the papers he had prepared that day and asking him more questions about the house he was buying in London.

Jonathan had made the offer on the house on the count's behalf, although at the time he had not understood how anyone could want the property. Carfax was an ancient and gloomy stone structure with an attached old chapel, which had been abandoned for years. Having now met the count, however, and having seen his current home, Jonathan realized that his new home would be perfect. Perhaps it was his ancient Transylvanian roots, Jonathan thought, but the count seemed meant for shade and shadow.

Every night the count kept Jonathan up and talking almost until dawn. It seemed strange at first, but Jonathan quickly got used to it. After all, he thought, some people were just night people and, as he was here on a job, he had to adjust to his client's schedule.

Every day Jonathan woke up late, showered, used his little mirror to shave, ate a quiet breakfast alone, and worked on his papers. Occasionally he would write in his little journal, which, out of force of habit from childhood, he kept hidden on his body. Sometimes he wrote letters to his boss, Mr. Hawkins, or to his fiancée, Mina, but Jonathan dared not write anything too personal, and certainly not to write in shorthand, which Mina understood. This was because the few envelopes the count gave him for his personal use were so thin anyone could see right through to what was written on the paper inside. Just as speaking a foreign language in front of someone who did not understand could seem rude or suspicious, so might writing in shorthand, Jonathan thought. It was a dull routine, but then work was not necessarily meant to be exciting. And besides, soon some things would happen that would make him long for a dull life once more.

First, the count casually mentioned that Jonathan would be staying on at the castle for at least another month. Jonathan frowned. It seemed strange that this was such a long project.

Seeing Jonathan's face, the count frowned, too. "That is what I want, and I will take no refusal. Your employer assured me that my needs would be met. Is there going to be a problem?"

Jonathan forced his face to go blank. "No, of course not. I will stay as long as you need me."

The next thing that happened was even more upsetting. Unable to sleep one night, Jonathan hung his shaving mirror on the wall and was trying to shave when he heard the count say "Hello" directly behind him. Jonathan jumped, not so much because the count had surprised him as because he realized that the count's reflection did not appear in the mirror. What kind of strange magic was this?

Spotting the mirror, and himself not in it, the

count's eyes blazed with fury, and he made a sudden grab for Jonathan's throat. When his hands touched the rosary beads that held the crucifix Jonathan wore, however, the count pulled away almost violently. But he was not finished. Muttering something about vanity, the count opened the nearby window and flung the mirror outside. Somewhere far in the ravine below, the glass shattered into a thousand pieces.

"So sorry about that," the count said, "but mirrors are not a good idea out here. They are so

likely to break and cut people, and cuts are a dangerous thing in the country. Risk of infection, you know."

The last thing that happened was that, while exploring the house a bit further one day while the count was out, Jonathan realized that all of the doors to the outside were locked. Unless he went through one of the windows, plunging like his poor mirror into the deep ravine below, there was simply no way out of this castle.

The castle was a prison, he realized in horror, and he a prisoner in it! The townspeople had been right. What kind of a monster was this, he wondered, who did not even appear in mirrors? Oh, those wonderful townspeople, Jonathan thought. Thank God he had at least accepted their crucifixes and their garlic! If only he had accepted their wise and well-meaning advice.

CHAPTER 4

The Ladies and the Lizard

At first Jonathan panicked, feeling like a rat in a trap.

After a while, however, he forced himself to quiet his mind. He knew he needed to be calm to plan his escape. Most important, he thought, he must not let on that he knew. He was a prisoner who must pretend to be a guest, but all the while he would remain watchful, gather information, and try to formulate a plan.

Every night, while only he ate, he forced

himself to calmly discuss business matters with the count. And during the day, while the count was away, he explored the depths of the castle further, trying to unlock its evil secrets.

One day, as sunset was approaching, Jonathan came upon a door at the top of a stairway. It seemed locked, but gave under a little pressure. Once inside, Jonathan looked around, thinking that this was probably the part of the castle occupied by the ladies in the olden days, for the furniture was more feminine than in the other rooms he had seen.

Sinking down onto some soft cushions, he could practically see the ladies who had once lived here, sitting on this very couch, writing love letters. As he let his mind wander, he began to grow very sleepy. Despite the count's warning, he decided that he would sleep here. Just for one night, it would be a sweet escape from his prison cell.

Was he still sleeping? He did not know. All he knew was that he was not alone. In the moonlight opposite him were three young women who appeared to be sisters. All very beautiful, they had ruby lips and white teeth, and they floated around him like mist.

"You go first," one of them said, leaning over him lower and lower.

She is going to bite my neck! Jonathan thought in alarm.

Before he could react, the count appeared out of nowhere. Furious, his eyes positively blazing, he grabbed the woman kneeling over Jonathan by the neck and threw her to the side like a rag doll.

"How dare you?" he hissed at the three sisters.

He spoke in a low voice, but Jonathan could hear him. "I told you, you may have him when I am done with him." Perhaps as a consolation prize, the count threw the women a big bag with something wiggling in it. They grabbed it up and, giggling, ran away.

What was in that bag? Jonathan wondered, in horror. *A cat or perhaps a dog?* He shuddered to think.

Returning to his room, Jonathan felt a brief sense of comfort, but upon opening the window to get some air he saw something that only made him feel more frightened. Jonathan saw the count emerge from his own bedroom window and climb headfirst, down the stone wall, with his fingers and toes gripping the stones like a lizard! Jonathan pulled back quickly before the count could see him.

The next evening, however, he wondered if the count had seen him after all, for that night he was given a strange new assignment.

"You must write three letters," the count said. "I will mail them for you. The first will say that your work here is nearly done, and that you will start home in a few days. The second will say that you will be leaving the following morning. And the third will say that you have already left the castle and arrived at the town of Bistritz." The count nodded. "Yes, the mail is not picked up very often. Given how busy you are, it really will be the best and most convenient thing for you to take care of all your letter writing up front."

Jonathan swallowed in fear. Why would the count be asking him to write these letters unless he was planning to kill him, and create a story to cover up his tracks? Of course, he could not show the count his fear. "What dates shall I put on the letters?" he asked casually.

"June twelfth, June nineteenth, and June twenty-ninth," the count said.

It was now May 19, Jonathan thought. He

now knew the span of his own life! God help him! Briefly he considered writing something else in the three letters and sealing them quickly, before the count could see, but he thought better of it. Thank God he had, for in addition to once again giving him thin envelopes, this time the count actually ripped open the seals to confirm the letters' contents.

In the meantime, however, Jonathan took a terrible chance. Having noticed some Gypsies outside his window in search of work, Jonathan decided that he would write one additional letter, to Mina, in shorthand, and try to get it outside to the Gypsies to mail. He would throw it out the window with a gold coin. He would not tell Mina everything about his situation, or she would die from fright, but he would tell her enough so that she could possibly help him, if only by sending Mr. Hawkins.

Attracting the attention of one of the Gypsies,

Jonathan threw down the letter and the gold coin, gesturing with his hands that he needed the letter mailed. The Gypsy seemed to understand and agree, and Jonathan breathed a sigh of relief.

The next evening, however, the count came into the room, sat beside Jonathan, and handed him the letter he had written to Mina. The letter had been opened. The gold piece, of course, was gone.

"One of the Gypsies outside gave me this letter," the count said. They found it on the ground outside and thought that I had accidentally dropped it, but apparently it is you who has had the accident."

Looking down at the letter, and seeing its strange shorthand symbols, the count became enraged, his eyes blazing wickedly. With a sharp movement, he turned and threw the letter into the fire.

"I know you won't mind my doing that," he said, "for surely that was a mistake and not truly your letter, written in some sort of made-up language." Then he turned and left the room.

The next day, upon returning to his room from a walk, Jonathan found that every scrap of paper and every pen had been removed, along with all of his money and checks. Even his suit and coat were gone.

Thank God he kept his journal on his body, he thought, or the count would have found that, too. But there was no denying it: He was even more of a prisoner now!

CHAPTER 5

Jonathan Explores the Chapel

The next day Jonathan heard a commotion outside his window and rushed to it. This time he saw not Gypsies but Slovaks, two of them, wearing dirty sheepskins and high boots and driving two great wagons drawn by eight sturdy horses.

Jonathan screamed down as loud as he could, until he was hoarse, but they would not look up at him. Jonathan could see that the wagons held large square boxes, resembling coffins, each bound by handles of thick rope. From the ease with which the Slovaks unloaded the boxes into the castle yard, Jonathan knew they were empty. After unloading the last box, the Slovaks touched their whips to their horses and were gone.

Over the next few days other men came. From what Jonathan could tell, the boxes were brought somewhere deep into the basement of the castle. Throughout the house, from down below, could be heard the muffled work noises of shovels digging through soil and rocks. What was going on?

One night Jonathan saw the count climb out his bedroom window and down the wall like a lizard again, only this time the count was wearing the suit of clothes that had been taken from Jonathan's room! Jonathan realized in dismay that the count wanted people to think they had seen Jonathan himself, to create further evidence to support the fake letters. It also frightened Jonathan that any wickedness the count might do while in town would be blamed on him.

Later that night Jonathan was awakened by

the sound of an agonized cry in the courtyard below. Rushing to the window, he saw a woman with messy hair, gasping from the effort of crying and running. When she saw Jonathan's face at the window, the woman lurched forward, pointed at him, and shouted, "You! Monster, give me my dog! Please! I beg you!"

Before Jonathan could respond to her, somewhere high overhead, probably in the castle's tower, he heard the harsh metallic whisper of the count, as though he was calling something. Jonathan watched in horror as the count's call seemed to be answered from far and wide, throughout the valley, by the howling of wolves. Within minutes a pack of them poured through the wide entrance into the courtyard like a pent-up dam that had broken.

Jonathan closed his eyes. He couldn't bear to watch. He didn't need to shut his ears, however, because there was no cry from the woman; there wasn't time. After only a few minutes the wolves streamed away. They moved quietly, licking their lips.

The next day was the date of the last of the letters the count had forced Jonathan to write. He didn't have much time. He had to come up with a plan!

He had not yet seen the count in daylight, he realized. Could it be that the count slept when others were awake? If only he could get into the count's room! Surely the answers to some of his questions could be found there. But how? The door was always locked.

He had an idea. If the count climbed out his window, maybe Jonathan could climb in that very same way and, somewhere in there, find the key to the front door. Of course, he could not scale walls like a lizard, but there were ledges on the castle's outside walls, and other stones that were roughly cut. Both could possibly offer a few nooks and crannies for human toes.

Later that day he found an open window that was on the same level as the count's and shared a ledge. Jonathan climbed out. While crawling slowly sideways, he looked down, but was so overcome by the height that he kept his eyes up after that. Upon reaching the count's window and slipping inside, Jonathan looked quickly around, in fear, for the count. The room was empty.

In fact, the room was barely furnished and covered in dust, as if it had never been used. In one corner was a heap of gold, also covered in dust, and all of which must have been hundreds of years old. At the far end of the room was a heavy door, behind which lay a circular stairway leading steeply down deep into the earth. Holding his breath, Jonathan pushed forward.

There, at the bottom of the stairs and through another long, stone passage, Jonathan found himself in an old, ruined chapel. The floor was made of soil, and seemed to have been used as a graveyard. There, all around him, were the boxes that the Slovaks had brought. Now, however, they were filled with freshly dug earth.

And in one of the boxes, of which there were fifty in all (Jonathan quickly counted), on a pile of newly dug earth, lay the count! He was either dead or asleep, Jonathan could not tell which. His eyes were open and his lips were as red as ever, but there was no sign of movement—no pulse, breath, or beating heart.

Glancing one last time at the count's cold deadish eyes, Jonathan turned and ran back up the stairs, through the count's window, out to the ledge and sideways, and back in through the window from which he had come out.

Returning to his room and throwing himself, panting, onto the bed, he tried to think. Tomorrow was the date of his last letter. What was he going to do?

∽

"Am I leaving tomorrow?" Jonathan dared to ask the count when he saw him later that evening, after he had obviously awoken from his nap in the box.

"Yes, my friend," the count said. "Tomorrow we will part."

"Why can't I go tonight?" Jonathan asked.

Surprised, the count replied that his coachman and horses were away on a mission.

"I would gladly walk," Jonathan said. He didn't care anymore if his fear was obvious. He wanted to get away. He had to get away!

"And your baggage?"

"I can send for it another time."

The count stood up and smiled diabolically. "Of course, I would not keep you for one hour in my house against your will. If you want to go tonight, by all means, you shall."

With a stately gravity, the count picked up a lamp and led Jonathan down the stairs and to the front door. Jonathan was so relieved that he felt he could run all the way back to London, if he had to.

As they approached the door, however, a familiar sound started to build. It was the howling of the wolves from the valleys down below, growing louder and louder, just as it had on that night when the woman had come looking for her stolen pet.

As the count put his hand on the door's great handle and pulled, Jonathan could see that, indeed, the wolves were right outside the front door, leaping and licking their chops, just waiting for him to step outside. Only the count's body stood between him and his death.

"Shut the door!" Jonathan cried. "I shall wait until morning!"

"As you like," the count said serenely. "I just want my guests to be happy."

Jonathan did not breathe easily again until the rooster crowed the next morning. He ran straight to the front door and tried to open it, but the door would not move. Despair seized him and he pulled and pulled, but the door had been locked again from the inside with a key—a key that the count probably carried on his body.

Jonathan turned. He knew he had to get back into the count's room again, and then down into that dungeon, to find an escape.

The earth box was in the same place, but the lid had been laid on it, with nails not fastened but set in place as if someone was about to do so. Raising the lid, Jonathan saw the count.

Something was different. Now the sleeping monster looked twice as young. His white hair and mustache had turned dark iron gray, and his previously pale cheeks now seemed fuller and almost pink. Finally, his mouth was redder than ever, and on his lips Jonathan could see faint traces of blood. The count had been drinking it, and this was the effect.

Looking at the mocking smile on the count's sleeping face, Jonathan realized that this was the creature he was helping to transfer to London, where perhaps for centuries to come he might terrorize that city and create a new circle of semi-demons, like the three women, to prey on the helpless.

He couldn't let that happen. Looking around, he saw a shovel that the workmen must have used to fill the boxes. Lifting it high, Jonathan struck downward, as hard as he could, at the count's hateful face. But just as he did so, the count's head turned and its eyes fell upon Jonathan, seeming to stare right at him. Distracted, Jonathan missed his mark, still hitting the count in the head but merely making a slight gash in his forehead.

He couldn't do it. After all, he was not a monster himself. In the distance, then, he heard a Gypsy song sung by merry voices coming closer. Over their song came the rolling of heavy wheels and the cracking of whips. It was the Slovaks, returning.

Soon the sounds were even closer, seeming to come from inside the house. Running up the stairs from the dungeon, Jonathan waited inside the count's room, which was also locked from the inside, determined to rush out the instant the door to the hallway was opened.

However, the sounds suddenly seemed to be coming from down below, in the chapel. There must be some other way in, Jonathan realized, from the outside. He tried to run back down into the chapel basement, but at that moment a puff of wind sent the door to the winding stair shut with a loud boom. When he tried to open it, it was shut fast.

From down below came the sound of hammering, many trampling feet, and heavy objects being moved. It was the sound of the count's box being nailed closed and of the Slovaks taking that box and the other boxes of earth out of the castle. Running to the window and looking out, Jonathan could see the wagons, heavily loaded, beginning their caravan out of the courtyard.

It was too late. The count was gone, on his way to London, and Jonathan was alone here in the castle with the awful women. It was too much to bear, he thought. He had to get away from this evil place, where the devil and his children walked with earthly feet. He would escape even if it meant plunging to his death. Jonathan opened the window and began to climb.

CHAPTER 6

The Storm Brings a Strange Ship to Whitby

❦

Mina Murray, Jonathan's fiancée, was worried. He had been away for so long now, and had written her only a few times, which was very unlike him. Also unusual was the way he had written— stiffly, formally, and in longhand, instead of the shorthand he usually used.

He was probably just busy, she figured, and she tried not to worry. Besides, Jonathan's last letter did state quite clearly that he was well and would be returning in about a week. She couldn't wait to hear all about his adventures in Transylvania.

In the meantime, today Mina would be distracted by a welcome visit from her good friend Lucy Westenra. Lucy had recently been presented with not one but three marriage proposals, and she was eager to tell Mina all about it.

The first proposal was from a Dr. John Seward, a kind and smart man who managed a small lunatic asylum in a home in town, where he lived as well. She did not love him and so she had told him no.

The second proposal was from a very nice American from Texas, a Mr. Quincey P. Morris. Perhaps because he was so jolly, it had been easier to reject Mr. Morris than Dr. Seward.

The third proposal was from Mr. Arthur Holmwood. Tall, handsome, and curly-haired, and a longtime friend of the family, Mr. Holmwood had actually introduced Lucy to the other two men. It was he, however, who had stolen her heart. His was the only proposal that she could accept.

To celebrate, and to plan the wedding, the women were going away on a little vacation. They would be staying in Whitby, an old whaling village, in a little inn with a view of the harbor and the bay.

Whitby was a beautiful, gloomy old town. By the bay, part of an old cemetery on a cliff had slipped into the sea, leaving some of the headstones askew, like a sad sculpture garden. Being somewhat dramatic in nature, Lucy was particularly drawn to the old cemetery. The two women sat there for hours, using one of the sideways-pushed headstones as a seat, sometimes not even speaking, so content were they with their thoughts and their books.

Other times they would have company, in the form of the occasional interesting town character. Some of these people shared superstitious tales. If a bell rang, for example, they said it meant a ship was lost at sea. One old man, a Mr. Swales, would always scoff at such things, dismissing them as silly ghost stories.

As their vacation progressed, however, instead of relaxing, both women seemed to grow more stressed. To begin with, after the last of his three strangely brief and formal letters, there had been no further word from Jonathan. What's worse, contrary to what he had promised in his letters, he had not yet returned to London.

Lucy, too, was making Mina uneasy. She had reverted to her old childhood habit of sleepwalking. Mina forced herself to try to sleep lightly so that she would awaken at the sound of her friend wandering around and could gently lead Lucy back to her own bed.

Even the weather seemed to be growing

worried. The local fishermen predicted they were in for a storm. Even old Mr. Swales had to admit it. Pointing out to sea one day, he shivered and said, "There is something in the wind that sounds, looks, and tastes like death."

Perhaps it was the strange ship out there, which many in the town had lately noticed, steering very curiously and changing course with every puff of wind.

The fishermen were right, and the storm that eventually came into Whitby was one of the greatest storms ever recorded. On the day the tempest swept into town, the sunset had been simply glorious, and most of the townspeople had come out to the cliffs to take in the splendid colors. All present also noticed the strange ship still out there in the harbor and still flying full sails, which was extremely dangerous in the rapidly building wind.

Shortly after midnight a strange sound came

from out over the sea. Without warning, the sky exploded. The waves rose furiously and turned the sea into a devouring monster. Masses of heavy sea fog came rolling inland. Wet white clouds danced like ghosts. Thunder boomed, lightning flashed, and the townspeople huddled together and held their breath as, one by one, the boats still at sea made it safely to port, to cheers.

Eventually, only the strange boat remained out there, sails still fully set. It now seemed in danger of missing the harbor entirely and splintering into pieces on the sharp reef just beyond. Then, miraculously, the wind shifted and the ship was blown into the harbor, driving itself violently up onto a sand barge but otherwise remaining intact.

When the townspeople approached the ship the first thing they saw was a corpse, with a drooping head, its hand tied with ropes onto the helm, the stick that steered the ship. There was

no other living soul on board. The ship had been steered by a dead hand!

"What's that he's holding?" one of the townspeople asked. Someone hopped aboard to see. It was a crucifix, and from the shape of the crucifix pressed into his hand the captain had been clutching it tightly.

Everyone gasped as an immense dog sprang up out of nowhere from belowdecks, jumped off the boat, and ran through the crowd and into the darkness toward the cemetery.

CHAPTER 7

Dr. Seward's Most Interesting Patient

༈

As a doctor, the recently rejected John Seward knew that one of the best cures for heartbreak was work. Yes, that's what he would do: throw himself into his work at the lunatic asylum. One patient in particular was so interesting that he would provide the perfect distraction.

The patient's name was R. M. Renfield, and he was a most unusual lunatic. He had great physical strength and his moods swung wildly, from periods of great gloom to incredible excitement. He was selfish, secretive, and seemed to have a strange hidden purpose. Dr. Seward was determined to discover it.

Renfield's only good quality, or so it seemed, was his love of animals, including even such despised creatures as flies and spiders. Renfield lured so many of them into his room through his window, that Dr. Seward had to draw the line.

"You must get rid of the bugs," he said, gently.

Surprisingly, Renfield agreed. In fact, when a particularly fat fly flew by at just that moment, Renfield decided to get rid of it right then and there. Catching the fly, he put it between his finger and thumb and, before Dr. Seward could stop him, ate the bug.

Disgusted, Dr. Seward scolded Renfield for what he had done. Renfield, however, replied that the bugs were alive and therefore when he ate them, they gave that life to him. Days later, Dr. Seward saw with some pity that Renfield had a new pet, a chubby sparrow probably lured in by the few remaining bugs. Indeed, Renfield ate that sparrow, too. The doctor was certain he had gone too far when he asked next for a cat.

"Absolutely not," Dr. Seward replied.

One night Dr. Seward went to interview Renfield, but he was not in the mood to talk. Excited and distracted, all he would say was, "Ah, yes, finally, the Master is at hand, the Master is at hand."

Later that night the attendant came to wake Dr. Seward. Renfield had escaped, going out his hospital window. Dr. Seward threw on his clothes immediately. Renfield was far too dangerous to be roaming freely about.

Once he was outside, Dr. Seward saw Renfield scaling a wall in the distance, running toward

Carfax, a nearby estate. After going over the wall himself, Dr. Seward spotted Renfield at the door to the part of the house that had once been a chapel. As Dr. Seward grew closer, he could hear the following:

"I am here, Master. Now that you are near, I await your commands."

The attendant caught up with him and, together, the two men grabbed Renfield, who fought like a tiger, more beast than man. Eventually they got him back to the asylum.

"I shall be patient, Master," was the last thing they heard before they closed the door to the cell. "You are coming!"

After his escape, Renfield remained in a strange state. He was incredibly violent all day, and then extremely quiet from moonrise to sunrise. A few days later, the patient escaped again, running straight back to Carfax and pressing himself once more against the chapel door.

Renfield struggled as they caught him, only calming down upon spotting something in the distance. Turning to look, Dr. Seward saw a big bat flapping its silent and ghostly way to the west.

CHAPTER 8

Lucy Sleepwalks to the Cemetery

༺ঔ༻

The storm left Whitby as quickly as it had come, as though it had accomplished its one and only purpose. It turned out the strange ship was Russian, called the *Demeter,* and carried a very unusual cargo—a number of great wooden boxes filled with dirt. Members of a firm came by a few days later with papers proving that they had been hired to pick up and transport the boxes. The police authorized their removal.

In the dead captain's pocket, the police found a bottle containing a note. Written shortly before he died, the note told a tale of a fearful crew whose members had gone missing one by one. Someone had reported seeing a tall, thin, pale man—not one of them—aboard. A search, however, revealed no one.

The note told of fog growing and engines failing and still more men disappearing. Finally only the captain and one man were left, a Romanian who claimed not only to have seen the tall, pale stranger but to have stabbed him with a knife— only to have the blade slice right through him, as if through air!

"He is probably hiding in one of those boxes!" the Romanian concluded, vowing to go down and search every single case. Only a few minutes later, however, the captain heard a horrible scream followed by the Romanian running back up on deck.

"Save me!" he had cried, according to the note in the captain's pocket, his eyes bulging with fear. The captain had watched with horror as the

Romanian ran to the rail and threw himself to his death in the cold water below, claiming that only the sea could save him now.

Finally, the note related, the captain saw the pale man, too. "But I will not leave my wheel," the note concluded. "No matter what happens, this evil monster cannot make me!"

No one knew what to make of the note. Had the captain been insane?

The entire town attended his funeral, except, that is, for poor Mr. Swales. He had been found dead that morning, sitting on the women's favorite seat in the cemetery. He had died of fright, the doctor said. His face still had the expression of someone staring at something horrible. What could he have possibly seen?

The night of the funeral, Mina was so tired that she slept deeply and did not hear Lucy get up and sleepwalk down the stairs and outside.

When Mina awoke she found her friend gone.

She had a feeling where Lucy could be. Grabbing a heavy shawl, she ran toward the cliffs and the cemetery. Sure enough, as she approached and the moon peeked out from behind a cloud, she could see her friend in the distance, pale in her white nightdress, sitting upon their favorite headstone seat.

But what was that behind her, that long, dark thing seeming to bend over her? A shadow from a cloud? Some kind of man or beast? Mina ran as fast as she could and, upon arriving, confirmed it: Something long and dark was bending over her half-reclining friend.

"Lucy!" she cried, and the dark thing raised its head, revealing a white face and red, gleaming eyes. Or perhaps she herself was sleepwalking and dreaming? The clouds momentarily hid the moon again, making everything dark. When the moon came back, the monster was gone, and Lucy was still asleep. Mina shook her gently

awake, and Lucy moaned and put her hand to her throat. She had probably caught a sore throat, Mina thought, from the chilly night air.

Giving Lucy her shawl and pinning it at her friend's throat with a safety pin, Mina led Lucy back to the inn. The next day Lucy seemed fine, except for two little pinpricks on her throat.

"I'm so sorry," Mina said. "I must have pricked you with my safety pin."

"Don't worry," Lucy said. "I didn't feel a thing." But Mina was worried, for, over breakfast, Lucy described what she was certain must have been a dream, featuring the same long, dark figure with red, gleaming eyes that Mina herself had seen.

That night Mina locked the door to their room and kept the key on a string around her wrist, so that Lucy could not find it and leave the inn again. Lucy tried another route, however. Mina was awakened in the middle of the night by the sound of the window latch being opened.

Mina went to get her friend and pull her away from the window. There, in the sky between them and the moon, she could see a giant bat coming and going in great whirling circles.

"Go back to your bed," Mina said, shivering, and the sleeping Lucy obeyed.

Every night after that, Lucy continued to sleepwalk to the window. Once there, she would fall asleep, her head resting on the sill. One night Mina was awakened by a cold gust of wind and sat up to see her friend sleeping there with a giant black bird sitting right near her friend's neck.

As the days progressed, Lucy grew paler and paler, possibly from the chill night air. And, upon catching a glimpse of her friend's neck one day, Mina noticed with concern that the pinpricks, far from healing, seemed to have gotten worse! If they did not heal soon, she would insist that Lucy see a doctor.

CHAPTER 9

Jonathan Gets Better,
and Lucy, Worse

∽

How bittersweet! And yet, also, what sadness. Mina had finally heard some word about Jonathan, in the form of a note from Mr. Hawkins, Jonathan's boss.

According to the note, Jonathan had been ill in a hospital in Budapest for the past six weeks. Unable to communicate clearly, he had been suffering from some sort of brain fever, raving about wolves and poison and blood, about ghosts and demons. The nurses had not known quite what to make of it, but they were patient with him, and nursed him back to health.

Mina left for Budapest at once. When she arrived at the hospital and saw her fiancé, she almost gasped. Jonathan was incredibly weak and pale.

"Oh, Mina," he said, starting to cry. "If you will still marry me, we can have no secrets between us. I cannot really remember what happened to me before I arrived here, but I know that I must have written about it in my journal. The nurses tell me they found it on me when I arrived."

Handing her the tiny book, Jonathan said, "My secrets are contained between this book's covers. Read it if and when you must."

Mina took the book and put it away without opening it. She agreed to marry Jonathan and they had the ceremony that very day, with him still in his hospital bed. They had wasted enough time!

Meanwhile, back in London, where Lucy had returned when Mina had left Whitby for Budapest, Lucy continued to suffer from the strange dreams that had haunted her at Whitby. She could never really remember the details, but always woke up full of fear. Her face was growing ever more ghostly pale, and her throat hurt more and more each day.

Arthur Holmwood, Lucy's fiancé, was very concerned and asked his friend Dr. John Seward to come for lunch to see what he thought. "Don't tell her why you are here," Arthur asked.

John Seward could see that Lucy was very much altered. He told Arthur that he would like to write to his old friend and teacher, the great doctor and professor Van Helsing of Amsterdam. He knew more about unusual diseases than anyone else in the world.

Arthur agreed, and Professor Van Helsing came. He seemed concerned but would not yet say why. Rather, he asked for some time to think about Lucy's case. In the meantime he asked Dr. Seward to keep careful watch over Lucy and record every detail, however small.

Lucy continued to get worse. When Van Helsing saw her next, she was ghastly pale, with practically no red remaining in her lips and gums. Van Helsing frowned and pulled Dr. Seward into the hallway. "We must give her a blood transfusion at once!" he cried.

Arthur volunteered to donate the blood and, within minutes, life returned to Lucy's cheeks. She sighed and moved her head slightly. The collar of her nightdress moved to reveal the red marks on her throat.

Seeing the marks, Van Helsing inhaled so quickly that his breath sounded like a hiss. Arthur didn't notice, but Dr. Seward did. He waited until he was alone with Van Helsing to ask, "What do you make of those marks on her throat?"

"I am not ready to answer just yet," Van Helsing said. "I must go back to Amsterdam tonight and consult my books. You must remain here all night and not let her out of your sight." He grabbed Seward's arm. "I mean it. You must not sleep. I will be back soon, and then we can begin."

"Begin what?"

"You shall see."

The men agreed not to tell Arthur too much, so as not to cause him more worry. After all, they were doctors, better prepared for such matters. As instructed, Dr. Seward watched over Lucy that night and the next. Relieved by the doctor's presence, she slept like a baby. Between the blood transfusion and the rest, she was looking as good as new after only two days.

Poor Dr. Seward, however, was a different story. On the third day Lucy took his hand. "No sitting up tonight for you. You look horrible, completely worn out. And as you can see, I am quite well again."

Dr. Seward hesitated, but he was so tired, and Lucy promised she would sleep in the room just next door to his with the door open so that he could hear her if she needed anything.

Dr. Seward was shaken awake the next morning by a frowning Van Helsing. "How is our patient?" he asked.

"She was fine last night," Dr. Seward said.

The two men went to check on her. Pulling open the blinds in the next room, both drew back to see Lucy more horribly white and weak looking than she had been two days earlier. She seemed to have barely a drop of blood left in her body.

"All our work is undone," Van Helsing hissed. "We must begin again!"

This time it was John Seward who donated blood. Feeling responsible, he watched with relief as the transfusion once again had an immediate effect on the patient.

The next morning Van Helsing brought Lucy flowers, carefully arranging them around her room.

"They are lovely," Lucy said, "but what is that smell?" Then she realized what the flowers were—garlic! "Is this a joke?" she asked.

"There is nothing funny about this situation," Van Helsing snapped. "And you will leave these flowers here, for the sake of others if not your own." Lucy looked frightened, so Van Helsing said more gently, "I'm sorry, I didn't mean to scare you. Will you humor me and accept these humble flowers from me? Will you even go so far as to wear a wreath of the flowers around your neck, and not remove them?"

"I would be honored to accept your flowers," Lucy said.

"There is just one more thing," Van Helsing

said. "Do not open the windows or doors to your room."

Lucy did not understand, but she agreed.

∽

The next morning the doctors Seward and Van Helsing met Lucy's mother down in the parlor.

"And how is our patient?" Van Helsing asked cheerfully. To spare her, the men had not let on about the seriousness of Lucy's condition.

"Well, she might not have been so well," Mrs. Westenra said, "but I fixed that."

"What do you mean?" asked Dr. Seward, nervously.

"Well, when I went in to check on her last night," Mrs. Westenra explained, "the room was filled with smelly garlic flowers and terribly stuffy, as the windows were closed. So I threw away the flowers and opened the window for some fresh air. Surely my daughter had a better night's sleep because of me."

Without revealing any reaction to Lucy's mother, the two men waited until she had passed and then raced to Lucy's room. Of course, it had happened again. Lucy was paler than ever. Something in Van Helsing momentarily snapped. "How can we possibly fight these devils?" he cried, a comment Dr. Seward didn't really understand. After a moment, however, he got ahold of himself and it was back to business. This time Van Helsing was the one to donate the blood.

Dr. Seward had to return to the asylum to check on some patients, so Van Helsing agreed to stay with Lucy. Arthur was away on business.

A few nights later, Dr. Seward was in his study, reading some medical books after dinner, when the door burst open and Renfield rushed in holding a knife. Before Dr. Seward could react,

Renfield had cut the doctor's wrist with the knife, causing a few drops of blood to fall to the floor.

The attendants came in and moved to tackle him, but Renfield was already down on the floor. Sickeningly, he was lying on his belly, licking up the blood like a dog. Dr. Seward went to sleep feeling extremely disturbed.

And he was even more disturbed the next morning by the delivery of a telegram, twenty-four hours late. It was an emergency message from Van Helsing saying he had to leave immediately for Amsterdam and asking Dr. Seward to stay the night with Lucy. Dr. Seward realized grimly that the note referred to the night before. Lucy had spent the night alone.

Dr. Seward rushed, with a sense of dread, to Lucy's family house. When he arrived he met a panting Van Helsing in the hallway. Sure enough, the two men found a scene of horror.

As Lucy would later describe it, upon finding herself alone the night before, she had taken comfort in Van Helsing's flowers, which he had replaced, being sure to arrange them around her neck before she retired. When she tried to close her eyes, however, the howl of distant dogs and a strange flapping at her window had woken her up.

She had felt so weak and nervous that she had asked her mother to come lie down with her. And within minutes, Lucy would explain, there was a low howl right outside the window. Then there was a horrible crash as a giant wolf jumped through the window, right through the glass.

In her fear, Lucy's mother had clutched at the garlic flowers around Lucy's neck, ripping them from her. But they would not save her: The wolf tore at her mother's throat, taking her life before rushing back through the window outside.

Lucy had sat there, terrified, alone with the dead. She dared not go out. She dared not move. She had simply prayed.

This time was Van Helsing's toughest battle by far. He was able to revive Lucy slightly with smelling salts, but she needed more blood, and both doctors had already given a transfusion.

"Will I do?" boomed a voice. When they looked up, they saw Quincey Morris, the Texan who had proposed marriage to Lucy. Arthur had asked Morris to stop by to check in on Lucy while he was away. Van Helsing completed the transfusion.

Lucy recovered again, but this time something about her was different. Perhaps it was something in her eyes, some new hardness? It was hard to say exactly. In addition, her teeth seemed to have grown slightly. This fact seemed to concern Van Helsing the most.

When she was awake, she would pull the garlic flowers close to her. But when she was sleeping, she pulled them from her, exposing her throat. Her teeth continued to grow longer. But soon Dr. Seward saw that her neck wounds had completely disappeared.

"Why, that's great news!" Dr. Seward cried, but Van Helsing came to a very different conclusion. "She is dying," he announced. "It will not be long now. Go and get Arthur. He must be told."

A heartbroken and confused Arthur bent over his bride-to-be, the woman he would now never marry. Seeing him, a sudden strength seemed to come over Lucy. "Oh, Arthur," she cried. "I am so glad you have come. Kiss me! Kiss me!"

She grabbed his neck and pulled him down to her with all of her sudden strength. Van Helsing ran over, grabbed Arthur, and hurled him backward, sending him flying across the room. "Not for your life!" he screamed. "For the sake of both your living soul and hers!"

A fit of rage passed over both Lucy's and

Arthur's faces, but in a moment it vanished from hers and she seemed grateful for what Van Helsing had done. "Thank you," she said. "Please protect him, and give me peace." Lucy's breathing stopped then. She was dead.

Arthur fled the room, angry and upset. Dr. Seward came over and stood next to Van Helsing, looking down at poor Lucy.

"Poor thing," Dr. Seward said. "What an end."

"No," Van Helsing replied. "It is only the beginning."

CHAPTER 10

Van Helsing Asks for Faith

⁓

Jonathan's recovery came even faster now with Mina by his side. Life, however, remained bittersweet. Mr. Hawkins had recently passed away and in his will had left them a beautiful old house in Exeter. They were grateful and happy, but they both missed Jonathan's old friend and mentor. And only a few days ago, they had learned of the unfortunate deaths of both Lucy and her mother.

Other strange things were going on in London as well, with nightly news reports of people being kidnapped and returning with small holes on their throats—bites of some sort. These certainly were scary and confusing times.

Professor Van Helsing had written Mina, asking if he could come and visit her in Exeter. Although Jonathan was recovering, Mina thought Van Helsing might be able to help him, too. There were times when he still seemed quite shaky.

For example, at Mr. Hawkins's funeral, in London, they were sitting there quietly when Jonathan had clutched Mina's arm and muttered under his breath, "My God." She had turned to see what he was looking at. There was a tall, thin man with a black mustache and pointed beard. His face was hard and cruel and his big white teeth, which looked all the whiter because his lips were so red, were long and pointed like an animal's.

"It is him," Jonathan muttered. "But how can it be? He has grown so young!"

Worried about him, Mina pulled Jonathan away from the funeral's crowd.

"Please don't be angry," she began. "But I must understand what happened to you when you were away. Jonathan, may I read your journal?"

Upon starting to read the journal later that day, it was almost impossible to believe what Jonathan had experienced. She rewrote his shorthand into longhand as she read. Just as she finished the last page, Dr. Van Helsing arrived.

Her questions for him would have to wait, for he had many questions for her about what had

happened to Lucy, especially at Whitby. Mina was an observant young woman who had kept a diary of her own, and Van Helsing asked if he could read it.

"Dr. Van Helsing," Mina said, "I would be more than happy to give you any information I can about Lucy, but will you please also help my husband?"

"Why, of course," Van Helsing replied. "What can I do?"

"I am going to show you something," Mina said. "It is a transcript of my husband's journal." She clutched the papers close. "But you must promise me that you will not laugh or judge him. The things he writes of . . . well, they are not ordinary things."

"Do not fear," Van Helsing assured her. "I am used to strange things." Van Helsing promised to take the transcript home with him to read.

A few days later Mina received a four-word telegram. IT IS ALL TRUE, the telegram read.

At the same time, back in London, Arthur Holmwood was struggling with his own awful realizations. Standing at Lucy's body with John Seward while the doctor prepared her for her burial, Arthur asked, "Oh, John, is she really dead?"

Even in death, Lucy looked strangely healthy. Something was going on, and Dr. Seward needed to know what it was. Later, when Dr. Seward was alone with Van Helsing, he demanded to know the full truth.

"You have no suspicions?" Van Helsing asked.

Dr. Seward shook his head.

"I am not surprised," Van Helsing said, "for you are a man of science. Sometimes for men such as you, things that cannot be explained except perhaps by magic are very hard to understand. For example, can you tell me why some spiders live only a few days and other great spiders live for centuries in the towers of old Spanish churches, and grow and grow until they can drink all of the oil in the church lamps?"

"Spiders?" Dr. Seward asked.

"And why does the tortoise live longer than generations of men?" Van Helsing continued. "Why does the elephant go on until he has seen several dynasties?"

Dr. Seward's head was spinning. "Look, Professor," he cried, "just tell me! Is this some kind of mystery illness, caused perhaps by the bite on her neck? Those people who were found in town with small holes in their necks—were they bitten by the same creature that bit Miss Lucy? I can't figure it out. Why do you talk of spiders and tortoises and elephants when what I need is for you to tell me what to do?"

"What you must do," Van Helsing said quietly, "is to believe in the very things you cannot. You must have faith. Can you do that?"

Dr. Seward promised to try.

CHAPTER 11

Lucy Changes Some More

ᥣᥣᥣᥣ

Van Helsing was pleased by Dr. Seward's promise. "I will give you one specific answer," he said. "The small holes in the local people's throats were not made by the creature that bit Miss Lucy." He paused. "They were made by Miss Lucy herself."

"Professor, are you mad?" Dr. Seward exclaimed.

"I can prove the things I say," Van Helsing said. "Come with me tonight to the cemetery." He took something out of his pocket. "I managed to get the key to the tomb."

Dr. Seward had never been more confused. However, he trusted and respected his old teacher more than anyone else in the world, so he agreed to go. He would try to believe. He would try to have faith.

In Lucy's tomb that night, Dr. Seward watched as Van Helsing unscrewed Lucy's coffin and opened the lid. The coffin was empty.

"Proof enough?" Van Helsing asked.

"Could have been a body snatcher," John Seward replied.

"All right," Van Helsing said. "I will give you more proof."

That night they waited for Lucy's return. Something white came through the trees, but it was not Lucy. It was a child. Van Helsing suspected that Lucy was not far away, and had probably been chasing the child. Luckily the child was not harmed, only tired and dirty and scared. Van Helsing felt their first priority had to be to take the child to the police, out of harm's way. "I think that is an excellent idea," said Dr. Seward. He was still not convinced about Van Helsing's theory about Lucy.

The next morning Dr. Seward returned with Van Helsing to the tomb, and this time Lucy was in her coffin. She was, if possible, even more beautiful than she had been while alive. Her cheeks were pink and her lips were bright red.

"Convinced yet?" Van Helsing said.

"Well," Seward said uncertainly, "maybe the body snatcher returned her."

"This is not the face of a dead woman." Dr. Van Helsing said. He pulled back Lucy's lips to reveal long, sharp white teeth. "But these are the teeth that have been biting the local people." As he spoke, he arranged some garlic around the coffin, and laid a crucifix around Lucy's neck. "All right, John. Here is the plain truth, all of it: Lucy was bitten by a vampire when she was sleep-walking. Now she is a vampire. And I must kill her in her sleep."

"Go on," Dr. Seward said, his mind spinning.

"I must drive a stake through her heart. I must do this to her first and then to the great vampire who did this to her. But not tonight. We need to break the news to Arthur first.

"Arthur!" Dr. Seward exclaimed. "We cannot tell him. He will not be able to take this news."

Van Helsing disagreed. "We have to tell him. He senses something is wrong, but does not know what. This leaves him filled with anger and worry. In that state he will never heal. He must know the truth."

The next night, as requested, Dr. Seward gathered Morris and Arthur and met Van Helsing at his hotel.

"Do you trust me?" Van Helsing asked the

three men standing before him. "Will you support me in doing whatever it is that I must do?"

John Seward, already knowing of the plan, silently bowed his head. Morris said, "I don't know what's going on here, but I trust the professor and swear he's honest, and that's good enough for me. I'm in."

Arthur was not as easily convinced. "I don't mean to be difficult," he said, "but I am a Christian and a gentleman. If you can assure me that what you intend does not go against either of those two things, then I will support you."

"I accept your limitation," Van Helsing said. "Follow me."

As Van Helsing led the men into the churchyard where Lucy was buried, Arthur grew more and more tense. "Look here," he said, grabbing Van Helsing's arm. "What are we doing?"

Van Helsing spoke directly. "We are going to go into Lucy's tomb and open her coffin."

"Absolutely not!" Arthur cried.

"Why?" Van Helsing asked. "If she is dead, there can be no harm to her."

"If?" Arthur asked wildly. "Do you think she might not be dead? Was there a mistake? Was she buried alive?"

"She is not alive," Van Helsing explained patiently. "But she may very well be undead."

Arthur looked as if he might cut off Van Helsing's head. "I warn you, sir," he said quietly. "I have a duty to protect her grave, and by God I shall do it."

"I have a duty, too," Van Helsing replied. "I have a duty to others, to you, and a duty to the dead, and by God I shall do it. All I ask is that you come with me, that you look and listen, and then decide."

Arthur agreed.

CHAPTER 12

Lucy Changes Again

ᢙ

It was just fifteen minutes before midnight when the group, consisting of Van Helsing, Quincey Morris, Seward, and Arthur, climbed over a low wall and reached the tomb. The professor unlocked the door, lit a lantern, and pointed to Lucy's coffin. It was empty.

Arthur winced, as if in pain. The professor, however, sprang into motion. First he closed the coffin, took a piece of communion wafer into his hands, crumbled it up and wet it, and made a sort of paste. He pressed this paste into the coffin's seals.

"What are you doing?" Morris asked.

"I am sealing the tomb with the communion wafer, that blessed holy bread. It repels evil. Now let's go wait outside."

The men arranged themselves in the bushes. "Shhh," Van Helsing warned. "Someone is coming."

The men crouched and watched as a white figure moved toward them. Instantly they recognized the figure as Lucy, but all were shocked by how altered a Lucy she was. Her old sweetness had turned somehow to cruelty, and her old purity to a new evil. Arthur gasped.

Van Helsing raised his lantern and shined the light on Lucy. In its glow the men could see that her lips were crimson with fresh blood.

When Lucy saw the men, she snarled and hissed angrily, like a cat taken by surprise. Her eyes blazed with evil. But then she changed course. "Arthur," she said, sweetly stretching her arms out to him. "Come to me." Arthur moved toward her as if under a spell, and Lucy lunged for him. Van Helsing was ready for her, however, and leaped between the couple, holding a gold crucifix. Lucy jumped back, her face contorted, and moved as if to rush back into the tomb.

When she got within a foot or two of it, however, she stopped, sensing the wafer Van Helsing had placed within. She turned, confused and enraged. Sparks seemed to be flying from her. If looks could kill, hers would have. She was a monster.

"May I go on?" Van Helsing asked Arthur.

Arthur fell to his knees. "Do what you need to," he said, weakly. He closed his eyes, thinking Van Helsing was going to kill Lucy now. Instead Van Helsing walked past Lucy, removed the bread from the coffin's crevices, opened the container, and stood back. With something that could only be described as relief, Lucy glided in, and the professor closed the lid.

"Tonight is not the time," he said.

The next day they went back and found Lucy asleep in the coffin. The men took one last look at the beautiful woman's still-bloodstained mouth. The smile that lay on her lips as she slept was a devilish mockery of her life's sweetness.

Quickly Van Helsing removed his tools from his doctor's bag, including a round wooden stake that had been sharpened to a fine point.

"When the victims of the bite become officially undead," Van Helsing explained, "they keep adding new victims and multiplying their evil. Unless stopped, the circle is ever widening, like ripples from a stone thrown into the water." He spoke gently to his friend. "Arthur, if I had let Lucy kiss you on that day when I first stopped her, or last night when you wanted to hold her again, you would have become a vampire, too.

"If we kill her now, however, the wounds of all of the people she has bitten so far will heal right away, as her power over them will stop. And we will free Lucy as well.

"Instead of growing more and more wicked each day, our angel will take her rightful place where she belongs, with the other angels. We are doing her a kindness, if you think about it."

"Then let me do it," Arthur said firmly. "Just tell me what to do."

Van Helsing explained that Arthur must drive a stake directly through Lucy's heart. "You must not hesitate," Van Helsing said.

And Arthur didn't. Within a second the terrible task was over, and in the coffin was no longer an evil monster but their old Lucy, in a normal body. The look of calm on her face comforted all

of the men as they looked upon her. Finally Lucy was at peace.

"Now you can kiss her," Van Helsing said. And, leaning down, Arthur kissed her on the forehead.

"Our work has only just begun," Van Helsing announced. "Next, we must find the author of all this sorrow and stamp him out. Will you all help me? Shall we work as a team?"

The men agreed that they would meet two nights later at the asylum where Dr. Seward worked and lived. Van Helsing would bring two other men. Jonathan Harker, Van Helsing said, had kept a careful journal of his encounter with the beast, which was going to come in handy in their hunt.

Shaking hands, the men vowed to keep pushing, together, until the evil was eliminated.

CHAPTER 13

The Men Exclude Mina

Van Helsing returned briefly to his home in Amsterdam, to consult some of his books, and Jonathan left to check on the cargo that had been removed from the *Demeter,* the boat that had arrived under such strange circumstances at Whitby. Meanwhile, Mina came to the asylum to visit Dr. Seward. She needed to hear the final details of her old friend Lucy's death. The story was wild and mysterious. If Mina had not read of similar events in Jonathan's journal about

Transylvania, she would have thought that Dr. Seward was crazy.

Both of them marveled at the coincidence they had learned of from reading Jonathan's journal, which was that Carfax, the count's recently purchased home, was right next door to the asylum. It was now clear to Dr. Seward why Renfield, his patient who had craved the blood of animals, had been acting so strangely.

In addition, it was becoming clear that at least some of the boxes filled with earth had been unloaded at the Carfax estate. An attendant had reported seeing a large delivery there the other day.

Soon everyone was present and ready to begin getting rid of the evil monster. There was Van Helsing, of course, the unofficial leader of the team; Jonathan Harker, the only man among them who had already faced the count; the cheerful yet dependable Quincey Morris; the smart and scientific Dr. John Seward; and Lord Godalming, a man of money and manners, both of which would surely come in handy.

"What about me?" Mina asked.

"Your brain is a match for any man's," Van Helsing replied. "But hunting vampires is no job for a lady."

Mina held her tongue.

While Morris went outside to gather the weapons, Van Helsing told the group some key details about vampires. Each time a vampire bit, Van Helsing explained, it grew stronger. It had the power to direct the weather, creating storms, fog, and thunder. It could command rats, owls, bats, and wolves. It could not be seen in mirrors. Just one vampire had the strength of many men. It could grow huge or vanish entirely.

"But we must not forget that we mere men are powerful, too," Van Helsing stressed. "We have science on our side. We have the freedom to think and act. And, the vampire has a few huge weaknesses. His power ends at the rising of the sun each morning. He can only change himself at exact sunrise or sunset. And he is frightened of crucifixes and garlic."

"What is the plan?" Arthur asked.

"We must find each of the fifty boxes and purify the earth inside with blessed wafers so that the count will not be able to return. And then we must find this monster, between dawn and sunset when he is at his weakest, and drive a stake through his heart."

They were interrupted by shattering glass. It was the window beside them breaking. Someone had shot a bullet through it. They ducked, thinking it was the count, but it was only a shaken Quincey Morris, down below. He explained that he had seen a big bat on the windowsill, looking in at the men, and had shot at it with a gun.

"Nice shot," Lord Godalming teased.

"When do we start?" Mina asked.

"We, not you," Van Helsing reminded her.

Mina began to protest but even Jonathan seemed in agreement. The men were determined to leave her out of it.

An attendant knocked on the door then, with a message for Dr. Seward. Renfield was demanding to see him.

"I would like to meet this Renfield," Van Helsing said. The others decided to come as well.

When the men entered his room, Renfield addressed Dr. Seward. "Dr. Seward," he said calmly. "I must leave the hospital at once. For the sake of others, you must let me go."

Van Helsing stared at Renfield intensely, suspiciously. "What is your real reason for wanting to be free tonight?"

"I cannot tell you," Renfield said.

Dr. Seward refused. Breaking his composure, Renfield threw himself on the floor and begged hysterically. "Oh, please, let me out of this house!" he wailed. "You don't know what you are doing by keeping me here. I can't tell you who will be hurt, but please, I beg you, I am no lunatic. I am a sane man fighting for his very soul. Please!"

Dr. Seward was torn. Renfield did seem better, at least before this outburst. However, he seemed to be confused about the count, calling Dracula his "Lord and Master." Dr. Seward was afraid of doing anything to help the count. "No," he decided, and that was his final answer.

"Just remember what you have done later," Renfield muttered.

"I hope I did the right thing," Dr. Seward said as the group walked back to his office.

"We can only ever do what we think is best at the time," Professor Van Helsing replied.

CHAPTER 14

Mina Fears the Night

⤳

While Mina stayed behind and sullenly went to sleep, the men left the asylum and crept next door to Carfax through the dark. Each carried a crucifix, some garlic, and a piece of sacred wafer.

They had skeleton keys also, which can sometimes, if jiggled properly, open many different doors. The bolt to the front door of Carfax eventually opened; with a push, its rusty hinges creaked and the door slowly gave way. Peering inside, the men could see that the whole place was thick with dust and masses of spiderwebs.

They crossed themselves as they walked over the threshold.

"You saw maps of this place when you were arranging the purchase," Van Helsing whispered to Jonathan. "Lead the way to the chapel."

Jonathan quickly found the boxes filled with earth that they were looking for but, counting them, the men saw that there were only twenty-nine, not fifty. Just then something started moving on the floor beneath their feet. Was it the count crawling? Other vampires?

No, it was rats—hundreds of them. The place was alive with rats!

Lord Godalming reacted calmly. Taking a silver whistle from his pocket, he blew. It was answered from behind Dr. Seward's house by the yelping of dogs. After a minute three feisty terriers came rushing through the open door of the house and into the chapel. They charged and barked wildly, and all of the rats scurried away.

The men searched the rest of the house, but found nothing. The count was not there.

"At least we were able to count the boxes," Van Helsing said as they made their exit. "We also gained a sense of the house"

The men agreed it was best that Mina had remained behind. They also agreed that they would not share the frightening details of their job with her. This was hard for Jonathan, because he and she had always been partners, but he would do anything to protect her, and so he went along with the plan.

When they returned to the asylum, Jonathan checked on Mina. He found her looking paler than usual, but otherwise she seemed well and was sleeping softly.

The next day Mina awoke feeling strangely sad and low-spirited. It must have been her horrible dream, she thought, shivering as she remembered it. There had been mist, a heavy smoke pouring in through the cracks of the door. The air had seemed to grow heavy and dank and cold. And then there were red eyes and a dark figure, bending over her.

Surely, she thought, this was just guilt over the part she had played in Lucy's death by bringing her to Whitby. The next few nights, however, she experienced the same thing, and felt even worse when she awoke. She was growing paler and more tired by the day. She asked Dr. Seward for some medicine to help her sleep.

Dr. Seward prescribed something and the next night Mina took it, but as it began to take effect, a strange fear overtook her. Suddenly she wondered if she might have made a mistake in taking medicine that would not allow her to wake up if she needed to. Suddenly she suspected that she might be safer if she was awake.

But it was too late, for sleep had come.

CHAPTER 15

Renfield Speaks

Jonathan was hot on the trail of the missing boxes of earth. He questioned various people, starting at the company the count had hired to ship and deliver the boxes. He learned the destinations of some of the boxes in many different areas of London.

Later, Jonathan learned that several boxes had been taken to a house in Piccadilly. By pretending to be the sheriff, he was able to get the exact address. Upon going there, he knew he had reached the right place, for it looked like it had been a long time since anyone had lived in this house. A FOR SALE sign listing MITCHELL, SONS & CANDY as agents had only recently been taken down and was propped up against the house.

Jonathan went to the agents' office. When asked who had purchased the house, however, all they would say is, "The house has been sold." When pressed, one agent said, "The affairs of our clients are absolutely confidential."

"Your clients are lucky to have such serious and loyal men at their service," he said. "My boss, Lord Godalming, will be disappointed, but he will simply have to accept this news."

"Lord Godalming?" the agent asked. Jonathan could almost see the agent's mind working as he weighed the name of such a noble and wealthy man. The agent shrugged sheepishly. "Well, perhaps an exception can be made, just this one time.

The house was purchased by a foreign nobleman, a Count Deville. He paid in cash. Beyond that we know nothing."

"How are we going to get into the house?" the men asked when Jonathan returned with details of the house in Piccadilly. They suspected they would find everything they were looking for there—all of the count's papers and deeds and keys.

"We can break in, just as we did at Carfax," Van Helsing said.

"I don't think so," Morris pointed out. "There, we had the night and a wall to protect us. It will be a different thing to break into a house in broad daylight, and in such a central location, on a sidewalk."

Van Helsing thought for a moment before asking, "If we were the owners of that house and we couldn't get in, what would we do?"

"We would call the locksmith," Jonathan said,

"and stand there with him while he picked the lock. It's brilliant, really. The police could walk right by but if they saw an official locksmith's truck and uniform, they wouldn't think to interfere!" The men agreed it was a perfect plan.

Meanwhile Renfield seemed to be acting stranger than usual.

"Would you like some flies?" Dr. Seward asked him, trying to analyze him. "Or spiders?"

"Spiders?" Renfield scoffed. "There is nothing in them to eat or drink."

"Drink?" Dr. Seward repeated, alarmed.

Renfield looked guilty, as if he had accidentally revealed something. He did not want to talk anymore. Dr. Seward gave up but found it interesting how the patient had become so nervous at the mention of drinking.

Then Dr. Seward realized it: Renfield had moved past just wanting to feast on animals. It was a human life, and blood, that Renfield was looking for! Dr. Seward could only conclude that the count had gotten to Renfield, and that some new plan of terror was afoot.

Later that night the doctor's worst fears were confirmed. An attendant came to tell him that something had happened to Renfield. Dr. Seward rushed to Renfield's room, only to find him lying on the floor, unconscious and horribly injured, bleeding from blows to the body, head, and face.

"Go get Professor Van Helsing," Dr. Seward told the attendant.

Arthur, Quincey Morris, and Lord Godalming came as well. Van Helsing had the patient quickly whisked into surgery where he performed an

operation to relieve the pressure on Renfield's brain. Later, the patient opened his eyes.

"Am I dying, Doctor?" he asked Van Helsing.

"You may be, so now is the time to tell us everything."

"He promised me things," Renfield said. "He made me do things."

"The count? Go on," Van Helsing said.

"But he was a liar. And so tonight, when he came again for Miss Mina—"

At this, every man in the room jumped with a start and came closer.

"—I fought him," Renfield continued. "He did this to me. He broke me." The effort of speaking then became too much for him, and the men left him alone.

"To think," Van Helsing said. "We thought we were protecting Mina by keeping her out of our plans. Yet while we were away, not protecting her, she suffered."

The men ran to Mina's room but found it locked. They had a bad feeling about this and broke the door down and burst in. What they saw inside made the hair rise like bristles on the backs of their necks.

On the bed lay Jonathan Harker, breathing heavily and looking dazed. Kneeling over him was the white-clad figure of his wife, Mina. And by Mina's side there stood a tall, thin man wearing black. The count. With his left hand, the count held Mina's hands. With his right, he pushed down on the back of her neck and forced her face down onto his chest. He was forcing her to drink his blood!

As the men entered, the count spun around, his nostrils flaring like an animal's and a hellish blazing look in his eyes. Throwing Mina to the side, he sprang toward the men to attack, but the professor was ready and raised a hand containing a wafer. The count cowered and all four men advanced, holding their wafers and crucifixes before them.

Just then, however, the moon hid briefly behind a cloud. In the darkness the count disappeared like a puff of smoke, leaving only a faint vapor trail behind him.

Arthur and Lord Godalming ran out the door, trying to follow. Mina began to cry, a horrible endless wail. Van Helsing stepped forward and covered her gently with a blanket. Her neck was bleeding. She had given blood as well as taken it.

Jonathan stirred then, waking up and looking around, confused. "What are you all doing here? What has happened?" He looked at his wife, at the blood on her neck and her mouth. "What does that blood mean?" he asked.

Suddenly the realization came to him. "Oh, no, no, no!" he cried. "God help us, not that, not my sweet Mina!"

At this, Mina only wailed harder.

Jonathan hugged Mina. The blood from her neck stained his shirt, and she pulled away. "Do not hold me," she sobbed. "I am unclean. I cannot touch or kiss you anymore. Oh, to think that the person who loves you most should now be your worst enemy, the one you must fear most!"

Arthur and Lord Godalming returned. They had seen no trace of the count. While outside, however, they had seen a large bat rise from Renfield's window and, upon running up to the patient's room, had found Renfield dead.

"Was the bat headed toward Carfax?" Van Helsing asked.

"No," Morris answered.

"All right," Van Helsing said. "Well, the dawn is close, so he will not be back tonight. We will continue our chase of him tomorrow. But for tonight—" He turned back to Mina. "If you think you can bear it, you must tell us everything you remember."

"I took the sleeping medicine you gave me," Mina said. "I fell asleep. And the next thing I remember, there was a white mist in the room, and I felt the same terror I had felt before and sensed some kind of presence. Jonathan was asleep next to me and I tried to wake him, but I couldn't. I looked around, terrified. Then, out of the mist there stepped a tall, thin man, all in black. I knew him at once from the description all of you have given, and from Jonathan's journal. The pale face, the long nose, the red parted lips with the sharp teeth showing, and—" Here she shuddered. "Those awful red eyes!

"I was about to scream but he told me he would kill Jonathan if I did. He said he would drink my blood and that it was not the first time he had done so. I felt my strength fading. There was nothing I could do.

"And then he spoke of all of you. He mocked you for trying to defeat him—he who had lived for hundreds of years before you were even born. He said he would punish me for helping you. My punishment, he said, would be that I would forever come to his call. When his brain said 'Come,' I would be forced to cross land or sea to do his bidding. To ensure his plan, he opened a vein in his chest and forced me to drink his blood! I had no choice! I could not breathe! My God! What have I done?" Mina began to rub her lips vigorously, as though to wash off the poison.

From then on, the men decided, Mina should always know the details of their plans. Only Van Helsing had some reservations. "Aren't you afraid," he asked Mina, "not for yourself, but for others, given what has happened?"

"No," she said. "If I sense even slightly that I may harm someone, I will die."

"You would kill yourself?" Van Helsing asked, quickly.

"I would if there was no friend who loved me enough to do it for me," she replied.

"Absolutely not!" Van Helsing said forcefully. "You must not die, by any hand, but least of all your own. Now that you have sipped from his veins, if you die before the count, you will not truly die. You will live forever, just as he is. No, he must die before you, and he will. You will live a long and happy life with your husband. You must struggle and strive at all times to live. Do you understand?"

"I do," Mina said.

"Good." Van Helsing turned to the others. "We have the whole day to hunt him down, to find more boxes of earth, and to sterilize them. Until the sun sets, the count will stay in whatever form he is now. He is locked within his own limitations. Let's get to work!"

CHAPTER 16

Mina Is Burned by the Bread

∽

The men decided they would go to the house in Piccadilly, and that Van Helsing, Dr. Seward, and Jonathan would remain there while Lord Godalming and Quincey Morris left to find the coffins at various other locations and destroy them. It was possible, Van Helsing said, that the count might show up at Piccadilly during the day in human form, in which case they would confront him then.

Mina, who was still too sick to travel, would be safe at the asylum until sunset. The men would be sure to return before then. Still, just to be safe, Van Helsing spread garlic and crucifixes around her room. He then took out a piece of sacred wafer and touched it to her forehead.

When the bread touched her skin, Mina let out a fearful scream that froze everyone's hearts. The wafer had burned into her flesh, branding her as if it were a piece of white-hot metal!

Everyone realized at once what that meant: The count had truly poisoned her, and she was well on her way to becoming one with him. Sinking to her knees, she cried, "Unclean! Unclean! I must now bear this mark of shame upon my forehead!"

Van Helsing tried to comfort her. "I know that scar will vanish just as soon as this monster that is still upon us vanishes, too. Your forehead will someday be as pure as the heart we still know."

Before heading to Piccadilly, the men stopped briefly at Carfax to sterilize it, scattering pieces of

sacred wafer into all the boxes there. And, once at Piccadilly, they followed the plan they had come up with. Lord Godalming pretended to be the owner, locked out of his home. The others watched from a park across the street as a locksmith picked the lock. The police actually passed by on the sidewalk and tipped their hats, wishing the burglar Lord Godalming and the locksmith a good day! It was all in how you acted, the men realized.

Once the men were inside with the door pulled closed behind them, they did a quick search. The count was not there, but they did find eight more boxes and sterilized them all. The ninth box was missing, but they found many important papers, as well as keys to other houses where more boxes of earth were being stored.

Lord Godalming and Quincey Morris headed out to destroy the remaining boxes at the other houses, and time seemed to crawl while Jonathan and Van Helsing awaited their return. To pass the hours, Van Helsing told Dr. Seward and Jonathan a bit more about the count. A long time ago, Van Helsing explained, this monster had actually been a wonderful man—a soldier, a statesman, and a scientist.

Van Helsing's story was interrupted by a knock on the door. It was a boy delivering a message by telegraph. Van Helsing opened the door and the boy handed them a piece of paper. It was from Mina.

LOOK OUT FOR D, the telegraph said. HE HAS JUST LEFT CARFAX AND SEEMS TO BE HEADED YOUR WAY.

"Let him come!" Jonathan cried. "I can't wait to wipe this brute off the face of the earth. I would sell my soul to do it!"

"Do not say such things," Van Helsing warned him. "No one is going to sell their soul. We are going to fight this thing head-on."

Morris and Godalming returned and

confirmed that the boxes of earth in Bermondsey and Mile End had been destroyed. But just then, the men could hear a key softly being turned in the recently picked lock of the front door.

Without a word the men instantly came together as a team and took their planned positions, their crucifixes and wafers held tightly in their hands. The seconds seemed to pass with nightmarish slowness. Soon, careful steps came along the hall. The count was clearly prepared for some sort of surprise.

With a single leap he jumped into the room, running past them like a panther before anyone could stop him. Seeing them, he snarled horribly and showed his teeth. Jonathan acted first, taking a knife and leaping at the count. But the count was quick and jumped backward, avoiding the blade except for a piece of his coat. Oddly, gold pieces fell from the hole and tumbled to the floor.

A strange look of hate and anger came over

the count's face. His pale skin became greenish yellow and his eyes burned. Suddenly he ducked under Jonathan's arm, scooped up some of the gold coins, and threw himself out the window, shattering the glass. Falling to the ground below, the count sprang up, unhurt, ran across the yard, and pushed open the barn door at the end of the property.

He turned to scream up at them, "You hope to outwit me! You think that by purifying the boxes you have left me without a place to rest, but I have more! My revenge has just begun! I have spread it over centuries and time is on my side! Your women have fallen already and through them you and others shall also be mine! All of you shall do my bidding! I shall be your master!"

With a scornful sneer, he entered the barn and shut the door behind him. The men ran after him and searched the barn, but by that time the count was gone. Van Helsing was not discouraged. "We have learned much," he said. "Clearly, he fears us, and he fears time. If he didn't, why would he hurry so? Why take those gold coins? We are making progress. We will make some more tomorrow. Only one box of earth remains."

The fear, of course, was that the one final box could remain hidden for years, and that Mina would get sicker and sicker until she was completely lost to the count. They were racing against the clock.

The men returned to the asylum where, that night over dinner, Mina made a surprising statement. She reminded them that while all of them were sad and suffering, the count was the saddest case of all. "Just think how happy he will be when the evil part of him is destroyed so that his good part can live on forever," she said. "You must be kind to him in this way, too." She paused, and for a moment the scar on her forehead seemed to glow as an ever brighter reminder. "I may need similar pity someday. And I hope you will not deny it to me. You must promise me that, should the time ever come when I am so changed that it is better for me to die, you will, without a moment's delay, do whatever is necessary to give me peace."

There was a horrible silence. Quincey Morris was the first to respond. "I promise you, Mina, I will not flinch from the terrible thing you have asked us to do."

"My true friend," Mina said, kissing his hand.

"And must I, too, make such a promise, wife?" Jonathan asked.

"You most of all, my dearest," she replied.

CHAPTER 17

Mina Reads the Count's Mind

∾

Mina had an idea. Because she was now connected to the count, she wanted Van Helsing to hypnotize her. Perhaps the connection could be used to the group's advantage.

He did it just before dawn, when Mina felt she could speak most freely. When she opened her eyes, after being placed in the trance, she was not the same woman. She was obviously under the spell of the count.

"Where are you?" Van Helsing asked.

"I'm not sure," Mina answered, in place of the count. "But I hear the sound of lapping water."

The count was on a ship! It made perfect sense. He was moving his last box of earth by water. The sun came up just then, and Mina woke up.

"Did it work?" she asked hopefully.

"It did," Van Helsing replied.

The men quickly set to work on Mina's latest clue. There were many ships in the great port of London, but at least they now had a lead. They knew what the count had needed those gold coins for: a ticket for the ship.

Jonathan stayed behind with Mina while the other men went to search the ports. They suspected that the count was trying to get home to Transylvania. Soon they confirmed that, aboard a ship named the *Czarina Catherine*, a tall man, thin and pale, with very white teeth, dressed all in black, had scattered some money about and asked which ship was sailing next for the Black Sea. A deal had been struck and a great box brought on board. The box was to be unloaded in the port of Varna and handed off to an agent there. Later, a curious fog had settled over the boat before melting as quickly as it had come. In that fog, the men now knew, the count had snuck aboard and into the box. The *Czarina* then set out to sea.

Over the next few days Van Helsing hypnotized Mina a few more times, and her visions continued to tell him that the *Czarina* was on the sea. Van Helsing was worried, however. If they could tell what the count was thinking by reading Mina's mind, the count might also be able to read her mind in return, and learn of their plans for him.

Mina had the same fear. "My dear," she said to her husband. "I am changing more and more each day. My connection to the monster grows stronger. You must continue to hypnotize me and learn what he is planning, but for your safety as

much as mine, you must never tell me anything
about your plans, not until the scar is gone from
my forehead."

It was decided that the group, including Mina
this time, would travel by land in search of the
count. They would take the Orient Express from
Paris and beat the count's ship to Varna. Once they
found the ship, their best hope was to go aboard
when the count was still in the box, between sunrise and sunset, when he could make no struggle.
They would kill him, then and there, as they had
killed Lucy.

During the hypnotism sessions on the train
and upon arriving first at Varna, Mina's responses
continued to indicate that the *Czarina Catherine* was
still at sea. Mina spoke of lapping waves, rushing
water, and creaking masts. Finally they got word
that the *Czarina Catherine* was about twenty-four
hours away and would arrive at Varna the next

morning. That day Mina became extremely tired and had her most difficult hypnotic session yet.

By noon of the next day, there was still no sight of the ship or any news of it. Mina, however, was feeling better. In fact, although the scar remained on her forehead, she felt almost herself again, as if she had been freed. That day's hypnosis once more turned up "lapping waves" and "rushing water." So the *Czarina Catherine* was still on the water, but where? The boat should have arrived at Varna long before now. Was the count escaping to another port?

Two days later the men received a telegram, confirming their worst fears. Instead of landing at the port of Varna, as they had expected, the *Czarina Catherine* had entered the port of Galatz that day, which was farther upriver. The men quickly sprang into action.

"When is the next train to Galatz?"

Van Helsing asked Mina if she would mind going to get the train schedule. While she was gone, he turned to Jonathan and told him of his fears. When Mina had been especially tired a few days ago, it was likely because the count had sent his spirit to read her mind. Van Helsing put his finger to his mouth, for Mina was walking back into the room.

Both men tried to look innocent, but it was as if Mina could now read their minds as well. "He used me, didn't he?" she asked. "He read my mind."

Van Helsing nodded.

"But perhaps you are a bit freer from him now," Van Helsing said, trying to make her feel better. "The criminal mind is a selfish one. Now that he has gotten from your mind the thing he needed to escape from us, he thinks he is done with you. He may not suspect, however, that you are not done with him."

On the train to Galatz, during more hypnosis, Mina reported a change. "Something is going on," she said. "I can feel it pass me like a cold wind. There are men talking in strange tongues, falling water, and, in the distance, the howling of wolves." The next day she reported hearing cattle, water swirling, and the sound of creaking wood.

They arrived at Galatz and learned from the customs officials that the count's ship had indeed landed. It had been met by some Slovaks who were to take the cargo the rest of the way, by water. But what water?

Mina looked at a map. "Based upon what you've told me I said in my trances," she said, "I think the river is narrow and the boat is open, being propelled by either oars or poles, and going upstream. Such sounds would not have come from a boat gently floating downstream. So, according to this map, it is on either the Pruth or the Sereth River. The Pruth is more easily navigated, but the Sereth runs as close as anyone could get to Dracula's castle by water."

"My wife is brilliant," Jonathan said, and the other men agreed.

Van Helsing's plan was this: Just as they had raced the count to Varna, they would try to beat him to Transylvania. Lord Godalming and Jonathan would get aboard a steamboat and set off after him by water. Quincey Morris and Arthur were to follow on horses, by land. And Van Helsing and Mina would follow Jonathan's original path when he fled the count's castle, through the Carpathian mountains.

"You propose to bring my wife into the very jaws of his death trap?" Jonathan asked the professor.

"It is the only way to save her," Van Helsing replied. "Indeed, it is the only way to save us all."

CHAPTER 18

The Group Closes In on the Count

ᖆ

It was not smooth sailing for anyone in the group, either on or off the water. Lord Godalming's boat was briefly delayed, due to a minor accident that occurred while trying to force their way up a rapid. And despite confirming that the count was still on the water, Mina was becoming more and more difficult to hypnotize.

As they drew closer to the castle, Mina began to sleep all day. At night Van Helsing would awaken to find her staring at him with very bright eyes. He feared that the curse of the place was upon her, tainted as she was with the count's spell. He had to believe in the strength of her will, however, and that her soul, at least for a little longer, was pure.

Still, Van Helsing made a small circle of blessed wafers around them at the spot where they stopped to camp for the night.

"Will you come out to the fire?" Van Helsing asked Mina. It was a test, for the fire was outside the circle.

"You know I can't," she replied sadly.

Suddenly the horses began to scream. Van Helsing walked back into the circle just as the mist began to whirl around. Van Helsing and Mina watched as figures began to form in the fog. It was the three sisters Jonathan had described in his journal.

Seeing her scar, the women smiled at Mina, calling to her, "Come, sister, come! Come!" But there was nothing but disgust in Mina's eyes, which comforted Van Helsing. He charged out of the circle, holding some wafers, and the women ran off. However, the evil sisters had not left empty-handed. The horses were dead.

Van Helsing left Mina sleeping within the circle and walked to the castle alone. Breaking in, he traced the path described in Jonathan's diary to

find the chapel. Somewhere, he knew, there would be at least three graves to sterilize, holding the three sisters. He found and took care of all three.

And then he saw it, there, in the darkest, deepest corner of the chapel: an enormous, beautiful old tomb. On it was but one word: DRACULA. Opening it and finding it empty, Van Helsing sprinkled in some broken wafers, banishing the count from his hundreds-of-years-old home. Forever.

When Van Helsing returned to their camp he found Mina, still soundly and safely sleeping in the circle. Just as he woke her, however, to prepare her to walk back to the castle, they heard the distant howling of wolves and some kind of commotion quickly approaching.

"There is no time," he cried. "Hurry, we must hide!" Van Helsing found a narrow hollow in a rock face, and both of them ducked inside. From there, they would be able to defend themselves from either man or wolf.

As high up in the mountains as they were, they had a clear view down. Venturing out briefly, Mina spotted something hurrying up one side of the mountain. It was a group of Gypsies, transporting a cart that carried a large, square box. The count! The Gypsies were racing against the sunset, as they had surely been instructed and paid by the count to get him home before the magic hour.

Behind that group, however, there were two other horsemen following fast. It was Quincey Morris and Dr. Seward! And on the other side of the mountain, where there was another path to the clearing, Mina saw two other men, her dear Jonathan and Lord Godalming, also on horseback, rushing to the scene. It was like a beautiful dance. When Mina told Van Helsing, he shouted with glee like a schoolboy.

Closer and closer, the Gypsies drew. Van Helsing and Mina remained hidden in the rocks, holding their weapons ready, determined the Gypsies would not pass. All parties reached the clearing at the same time. From opposite sides the hunters on horseback yelled, "Stop!" The Gypsies may not have understood the language, but there was no mistaking the meaning of that word, or the weapons being aimed at them.

Jonathan and Quincey Morris rushed at the cart. Jonathan, more than any of the others, seemed to have a strange power, a superhuman strength. Dodging the Gypsies' knives, he reached over to the great earth box, raised it up, and flung it to the ground.

Quincey Morris rushed to help, also dodging knives, but not as successfully. One of the knives pierced his side, and he began to bleed heavily. Still, he continued to fight. Together, while the others stood guard with their weapons, the two men pried the lid off the great box.

And there he was, the creature they had been hunting for all this time: Dracula. Lying quietly within the box, the count was deathly pale, like a wax figure. His eyes, however, were open, and they glared with the evil look they all knew too well.

Just then those eyes saw the sinking sun, and the look of hate in them turned to triumph. The count thought that he had won once again. Once the sun set he would be safe from any harm.

But not so fast! In that instant Jonathan and Quincey Morris attacked, piercing Dracula's heart and cutting off his head with their knives. Before their eyes, the count's whole body crumbled into dust and disappeared.

The Gypsies, frightened by the sudden disappearance of the dead man, turned and rode away for their lives. Even the wolves retreated to a safe distance, leaving the group alone.

Quincey Morris, who had sunk to the ground, leaned on his elbow, holding his hand pressed to his side. Mina noticed that blood was rushing through his fingers. She ran to him, as did the two doctors, but there was nothing to be done. With a sigh, Quincey Morris took Mina's hand and smiled at her sweetly.

"I am happy to have been of service," he said. Suddenly he laughed, pointing at her forehead. "Oh, look! It was worth it to see this. Look! Look!"

The setting sun's red rays fell upon Mina's face, bathing it in a rosy light. As they all followed the path of Quincey Morris's pointing finger, they could see what he was referring to. The scar was gone. Mina's forehead was as stainless as the snow. The curse had passed away.

Quincey Morris died then, a gallant gentleman to the end.

Seven years later Mina and Jonathan returned to Transylvania. They brought with them their son Quincey, named for their old, brave friend. Walking over the ground that was so full of vivid and terrible memories, with Quincey Junior's little hands in theirs, they could look back without despair, remembering the great things that people can do for love.

What Do *You* Think?
Questions for Discussion

༄

Have you ever been around a toddler who keeps asking the question "Why?" Does your teacher call on you in class with questions from your homework? Do your parents ask you questions about your day at the dinner table? We are always surrounded by questions that need a specific response. But is it possible to have a question with no right answer?

The following questions are about the book you just read. But this is not a quiz! They are designed to help you look at the people, places, and events in the story from different angles. These questions do not have specific answers. Instead, they might make you think of the story in a completely new way.

Think carefully about each question and enjoy discovering more about this classic story.

1. As Jonathan sets off for the castle, all of the townspeople seem extremely scared. Why do you think this is? What are you afraid of?

2. Why do you think Dracula was so angry to find Jonathan with a mirror? Have you ever made someone angry without knowing why?

3. When Jonathan realizes what a monster Dracula is, he tries to kill him. Why do you think he is unable to go through with it? What would you have done in his place?

4. Renfield says that he eats bugs because they are alive and eating them gives that life to him. Do you believe this? What is the strangest thing you've ever eaten?

5. Why do you suppose Mina is so concerned about Lucy's sleepwalking? Have you ever walked in your sleep? Do you know anyone who has?

6. Van Helsing says that the key to understanding Lucy's illness is "to believe in the very things you cannot." What do you think he means? Have you ever believed something even though it was difficult to accept as true?

7. Van Helsing says that the only way to kill Lucy is to drive a stake through her heart. Why do you think Arthur insists on doing it himself? Have you heard of any other ways to kill a vampire?

8. Why do the men want to keep Mina out of the hunt for Dracula? Do you agree with their reasons? Have you ever been told that you couldn't take part in something?

9. Dracula seems certain that no one can beat him. Why do you think this is? Have you ever known anyone like him?

10. Were you surprised that Jonathan and Mina returned to Transylvania after killing Dracula? Where is the scariest place you've ever been? Would you go back?

Afterword

by Arthur Pober, Ed.D.

༅

First impressions are important.

Whether we are meeting new people, going to new places, or picking up a book unknown to us, first impressions count for a lot. They can lead to warm, lasting memories or can make us shy away from any future encounters.

Can you recall your own first impressions and earliest memories of reading the classics?

Do you remember wading through pages and pages of text to prepare for an exam? Or were you the child who hid under the blanket to read with a flashlight, joining forces with Robin Hood to save Maid Marian? Do you remember only how long it took you to read a lengthy novel such as *Little Women*? Or did you become best friends with the March sisters?

Even for a gifted young reader, getting through long chapters with dense language can easily become overwhelming and can obscure the richness of the story and its characters. Reading an abridged, newly crafted version of a classic novel can be the gentle introduction a child needs to explore the characters and storyline without the frustration of difficult vocabulary and complex themes.

Reading an abridged version of a classic novel gives the young reader a sense of independence and the satisfaction of finishing a "grown-up" book. And when a child is engaged with and inspired by a classic story, the tone is set for further exploration of the story's themes, characters, history, and details. As a child's reading skills advance, the desire to tackle the original, unabridged version of the story will naturally emerge.

If made accessible to young readers, these stories can become invaluable tools for understanding themselves in the context of their families and social environments. This is why the Classic Starts series includes questions that stimulate discussion regarding the impact and social relevance of the characters and stories today. These questions can foster lively conversations between children and their parents or teachers. When we look at the issues, values, and standards of past times in terms of how we live now, we can appreciate literature's classic tales in a very personal and engaging way.

Share your love of reading the classics with a young child, and introduce an imaginary world real enough to last a lifetime.

Dr. Arthur Pober, Ed.D.

Dr. Arthur Pober has spent more than twenty years in the fields of early childhood and gifted education. He is the former principal of one of the world's oldest laboratory schools for gifted youngsters, Hunter College Elementary School, and former Director of Magnet Schools for the Gifted and Talented for more than 25,000 youngsters in New York City.

Dr. Pober is a recognized authority in the areas of media and child protection and is currently the U.S. representative to the European Institute for the Media and European Advertising Standards Alliance.

Explore these wonderful stories in our
Classic Starts™ library.

Oliver Twist

Pollyanna

The Prince and the Pauper

Rebecca of Sunnybrook Farm

The Red Badge of Courage

Robinson Crusoe

The Secret Garden

The Story of King Arthur and His Knights

The Strange Case of Dr. Jekyll and Mr. Hyde

The Swiss Family Robinson

The Three Musketeers

Treasure Island

The War of the Worlds

White Fang

The Wind in the Willows